A Bride For Seth

Book Two

Brides of Broken Arrow

Cheryl Wright

A BRIDE FOR SETH

Book Two
Brides of Broken Arrow

Copyright ©2021 by Cheryl Wright

Cover Artist: Black Widow Books

Editing: Amber Downey

All rights reserved. Without limiting the rights under copyright reserved above, no part of this publication may be reproduced, stored in or introduced into a retrieval system, or transmitted, in any form, or by any means (electronic, mechanical, photocopying, recording, or otherwise) without the prior written permission of the copyright owner of this book

Dedication

To Margaret Tanner, my very dear friend and fellow author, for her enduring encouragement and friendship.

To Alan, my husband of over forty-six years, who has been a relentless supporter of my writing and dreams for many years.

To Virginia McKevitt, cover artist and friend, who always creates the most amazing covers for my books.

To You, my wonderful readers, who encourage me to continue writing these stories. It is such a joy knowing so many of you enjoy reading my stories as much as I love writing them for you.

Table of Contents

A Bride For Seth 1

Dedication 3

Table of Contents 4

Chapter One 5

Chapter Two 12

Chapter Three 24

Chapter Four 30

Chapter Five 38

Chapter Six 43

Chapter Seven 50

Chapter Eight 54

Chapter Nine 60

Chapter Ten 66

Chapter Eleven 73

Chapter Twelve 78

Epilogue 87

From the Author 90

About the Author 91

Chapter One

Somewhere outside Halliwell, Montana – 1880

Abigail Taggart wiped a stray tear from her eye as she glanced down at four-year-old Mabel who lay asleep slumped against her as they traveled to their new home.

The death of her dear sister Grace was totally unexpected. Abigail should be celebrating the birth of her new nephew; instead, she was mourning the loss of both her sister and her tiny baby.

Living so far from town meant medical help was not forthcoming for some hours, despite the best efforts of those around them. By the time the local doctor arrived, it was too late. The babe was long gone, and his mother lost her battle not long after.

When her unscrupulous husband heard the news, he was devastated. The last Abigail saw of him was his back as he left the property more than a week ago.

Mabel groaned and resettled her head on her aunt's lap. She slowly opened her eyes and glanced up at Abigail. "Are we there yet, Aunty?" She rubbed at her little eyes.

It had been a big adjustment – for them both. Abigail could not help but feel sorry for the child. It had been difficult enough for Abigail to understand. How did you explain to an innocent four-year-old her mother was gone forever?

Now Abigail had to explain it to her new husband. Their proxy wedding had been a Godsend, but they'd married before the tragedy occurred. Now she wished she could take it back. The plan was for her to travel soon after the baby's birth. Little did she know those plans would abruptly change.

Soon after the funeral she'd packed up their meagre belongings and left a note for Mabel's father. He could collect his daughter when things calmed down for him. Abigail didn't blame him for leaving. He was in shock, just as she was. But his daughter had to come first, and it was obvious he wasn't in the right frame of mind for that right now.

As they pulled into the Halliwell train station she took a long shuddering breath. What would her new husband say? She said a silent prayer for his understanding and compassion.

***

Seth Adams paced the platform as he awaited the arrival of his new bride.

It had been some weeks since their proxy wedding, which meant he'd complied with his late father's will. Except for the fact her sister was almost due to give birth, she would have arrived far earlier. Abigail explained she was required to care for her young niece and would come soon after the birth – at a pre-arranged date.

That suited him perfectly. After all, he hadn't wanted to marry. He was happy living the life of a bachelor, and if it hadn't been a condition of keeping the property 'gifted' to Seth on his twenty-first birthday, he would still be single. What was his father thinking when he changed his will?

That much was clear, Seth decided. Father wanted to see each of his three sons married. Two down and one to go, Seth thought bitterly. What a terrible thing to do to his own flesh and blood. It was an incredibly cruel trick Father had played; making them believe they owned the land they'd been given when they came of age. Both he and Noah had worked their respective land for many years, believing it was legally theirs, only to recently discover it wasn't – at the reading of their father's will.

Seth glanced up as he heard the whistle of the approaching train. Soon his new bride would become a reality instead of a faceless name on a piece of paper.

As the train slowly approached, steam and soot filled the air, and Seth stepped back. Time seemed to stand still as the brakes screeched, bringing the large contraption to a halt. Suddenly, the platform was filled with well-ordered chaos. Passengers began to alight, family and friends arrived to collect them, and porters scurried about pushing trolleys filled with luggage.

Seth scanned the area trying to determine which of the many passengers was his bride. He breathed deeply trying to calm his nerves and slow his pounding heart. It was finally happening; he was about to meet his wife for the first time.

Seth knew little about her except she'd been living with her sister and brother-in-law, acting as a nanny to her young niece. With a new baby coming, Abigail felt she'd outstayed her welcome, and decided it was time to move on, but had no prospects.

He continued studying the alighting passengers, but so far saw no lone women who hadn't been claimed. An eerie quiet overtook the place and the entire situation felt surreal. His heart rate quickened. Had she changed her mind? He glanced up again to see two passengers still awaiting collection at one end of the platform. A single woman stood at the other end.

She fitted the description he was given, so this must be her.

Their eyes locked and he breathed deeply. Suddenly a small child stepped out from behind her skirts. This couldn't be his wife - her niece was to stay with her parents, not be brought to live with her aunt and her new husband.

His heart suddenly thudded. Had the unthinkable happened?

Seth stepped forward to introduce himself. "Abigail?" he asked, feeling as though his throat had closed over. When she nodded, he continued. "I am Seth Adams. Er, your husband." It sounded crazy when he said it out loud. They were married yet did not know each other, could have passed in the street without recognition.

The little girl clung to her aunt's skirt. Abigail reached down and picked her up, and the child snuggled in further as he approached them.

"Yes, I'm Abigail. I…" She glanced at the young girl, and the color drained from her face. Tears suddenly filled her eyes, but she seemed determined not to let them fall, blinking hard.

He leaned in silently and picked up her luggage. "We can talk later," he said quietly, as he guided her toward the buggy he had waiting outside. Although he already knew what she would say, that her sister and the babe had not made it. But where was her niece's father? Shouldn't he take care of his daughter?

As they reached the buggy, her steps seemed to faulter, as though tiredness and stress had finally overtaken her. It had been a long trip for her and the child, and no doubt a difficult one.

Only moments ago, he anticipated the transition from being a bachelor to becoming a married man. Suddenly he was a father with a ready-made family. It was the last thing he had anticipated, and Seth had no idea what that would entail. One thing he did know was the Good Lord would not give him more than he could handle.

"Give me...the child," he said quietly, as he helped Abigail up onto the buggy. Her arms tightened around the little girl in trepidation, and she studied him with wary eyes. Suddenly her grip loosened.

"It's okay, Mabel," she said quietly, and passed her over. Once his wife was safely seated, he handed the girl up, loaded the little luggage they had, then seated himself.

Seth lifted the reins and flicked them, and they were soon on their way to the *Broken Arrow Ranch*. Seth glanced across at the two strangers sitting next to him. His life was about to change dramatically, but he wasn't sure if it would be for the better.

Chapter Two

Abigail had to fight sleep. With Mabel sitting on her knee, she could not afford to fall asleep. What if she dropped her niece and she fell off the buggy? She couldn't bear to even think about it.

"We're almost there," Seth said, startling her out of her weary stupor. She glanced up as she noticed the large archway bearing the *Broken Arrow Ranch* sign overhead.

She glanced about, but there was nothing in sight, no buildings. How big was this ranch? She'd been told it was large, and she would never want for anything, but this property seemed far bigger than even her wildest imagination. "It's huge," she mumbled under her breath, and he chuckled.

"It is rather big, but it's divided between my two brothers and me." His arm came up and he pointed in the direction of a dot in the distance. "That's Noah's place. Ours is not much further."

Ours. Soon she would need to consider this place home. A home for both her and Mabel. At least for now.

She glanced about to find the property was green and lush, and there were plenty of trees about. A small creek ran through it, and no doubt supplied them with fresh drinking water. Hopefully, it wasn't too far from the house to cart water, but on the other hand, she had to worry about Mabel getting too close and... She couldn't bear to think about it and felt the color drain from her face.

"The creek is quite a distance from the building. The girl will be safe," he said, as though he'd read her mind.

"Mabel," she whispered. "Her name is Mabel." Her arms tightened around the child, and she hugged her tight, then kissed her soft cheek. He nodded and smiled tentatively. Right now, he probably thought her niece was only here for a few days, but the truth of the matter was, Abigail had no idea how long Mabel would be with them. It could be a few days, a few weeks, or heaven forbid, she could be here forever.

She swallowed hard. What would Seth think if Mabel were to become his daughter? She stared at his profile. He didn't seem the type to reject a four-year-old. On the other hand, she didn't know him.

"That's us," he suddenly said, pointing to another building that was a mere blip on the horizon. "We're nearly home," he said directly to Mabel, and chucked the little girl under her chin. Perhaps she was worrying about nothing. Abigail knew only time would tell.

It wasn't long before they arrived at what had been described to her in letters as a cottage, and Abigail sat stunned. The family cottage her brother was allocated as foreman was half the size of this one, and she'd thought it was quite large. Seth's home was far bigger, and it was in a better position too.

Her brother-in-law Pete's place had a creek running directly behind it, which was always a concern with Mabel. She moved swiftly and loved water. If they weren't fast enough, she could be found sitting on the edge of the creek, water running over her bare feet. She'd given Abigail more than one fright.

Hopefully, the creek was far enough away that she didn't even know it was there.

"Are you still worrying about the creek?" Seth's voice brought her out of her thoughts once more, and she nodded at his words. "Then don't. You can't even see it from here, and if it becomes necessary, I'll build a fence around the perimeter of the house."

"You would do that," she asked, choking back tears as the buggy came to a halt. "She won't be here long."

He reached up and lifted Mabel down, then helped his wife. Mabel was at the front door before either of them even knew she was gone. "She's quick, I'll give her that," he said as he stared into Abigail's face.

She had to drag her eyes away from his to seek out her niece. In spite of their short acquaintance, she felt drawn to this man she'd been married to for several weeks now. Things hadn't turned out as planned, but Abigail felt relieved she'd waited until after her sister had the baby. If she had left earlier, she dreaded to think what would have happened to Mabel.

She rushed over and pulled the little girl close, a shiver running through her. Abigail picked her up as she stood and felt Seth's eyes on her. "Is everything all right?" His words were gentle, as though he didn't want to intrude on a private moment the two might be having.

Abigail glanced across at him, but said not a word, instead nodding. She pushed the little girl against her shoulder while she waited for the door to be opened. It wasn't long and Mabel was sound asleep.

Seth indicated for her to follow him and led her to a room with a single bed. He leaned in and folded back the bedding. There she lay the small child down, covering her with the warm bedding. She glanced about as they left the room – the cottage was clean and tidy, which was quite unexpected since her new husband had been a bachelor all his adult life.

He led her outside again, presumably so they could bring in her belongings. When they reached the door, he suddenly swept her up. "It might be a little late, since we married some time ago, but every new bride should be carried across the threshold," he said as he stared down into her face.

"But I..." His fingers suddenly covered her lips.

"Don't deprive me of making my wife happy," he said, then swooped in for a quick kiss. He suddenly pulled back. "I'm sorry. I shouldn't have done that; I should have sought your permission first." He might have sounded guilty, but he had a huge grin on his face.

Her heart fluttered. It turns out her husband was a romantic. Is this what their marriage would be like? A series of romantic gestures? If so, she could hardly wait to get to know him better.

* * *

Mabel wandered out into the sitting room rubbing her little eyes. "Where am I?" she asked quietly, still in a daze.

"We're at our new home," Abigail said, wiping her hands against her apron, then squatting down to Mabel's level. "Are you hungry? I'm making pancakes."

"Yummy," she said, brightening up. "I love pancakes."

Seth watched the interaction between the two. They were more like mother and daughter than aunt and niece. Abigail had told him she'd been Mabel's nanny practically since the little girl was born, so it was totally understandable. "I love pancakes too," he interjected, hoping to get to know the pair better.

While Mabel slept, he and Abigail had talked. It had been difficult for her to discuss her sister's death, and he'd held her hands as she did so. He had tried to ignore the shiver that ran down his spine at the touch, but it was not easy. Neither knew much about the other, since his solicitor and family friend Theodore Black, better known as Teddy, had made all the arrangements.

Getting married was not on Seth's list of things to do for some time yet, but if he didn't marry, his eldest brother, Jacob, would inherit his property. Jacob didn't want that, and neither did Seth. He'd had to concede to the marriage, and here he was now, with a total stranger in his house cooking supper. Tonight, those two strangers would share a bed since Mabel would sleep in the only spare bed there was.

"Supper is ready," Abigail suddenly announced.

Seth quickly set the table while his wife dished up, then helped Mabel up onto a chair. She was far too low to be able to eat, so he stacked the chair with cushions. He made a mental note to build some sort of platform to lift her higher. Once Mabel was sorted, he took his seat.

Abigail placed his meal in front of him; the aroma was enough to make his mouth water. Seth stared down into his plate. It was stacked high with fluffy pancakes, and to the side sat a mixture of fried potatoes, bacon, and onions. He leaned in and immersed himself in the

A Bride For Seth

delicious fragrance. He was about to tuck in when Abigail cleared her throat.

"You do say grace, right?" She pinned him down with her gaze.

Their eyes met. "Of course," he said, knowing it wasn't completely true. It wasn't a lie either – he did say a prayer of thanks on occasion but felt silly saying it when he was alone. Why, he had no idea.

"It's my turn, Aunty," Mabel suddenly said, and they both turned to look at her. They all linked hands and Seth wondered what was about to follow. "Bless this food and everyone sitting at this table. Amen." The words were said slowly and carefully.

Seth sat stunned. For a four-year-old, she did really well. "You did a wonderful job," he said, still in shock.

"Aunty Abigail teached me."

That made him smile. Now she sounded more like a child her age. Abigail squeezed his hand. Until that moment he hadn't realized their hands were still linked. "Now we can eat." He liked the sound of her voice. She spoke quietly and with respect. Abigail leaned over and cut Mabel's food for her, then they all began to eat.

"Mmmm, this is delicious!" It wasn't that he never had a home-cooked meal. Noah's wife Mary often invited him and Jacob over for a meal. He couldn't recall having pancakes there, so perhaps that was the reason.

"It's only pancakes. What do you normally eat?"

He glanced up. "Depends. I sometimes eat at Noah and Mary's place. She's a great cook. When I cook for myself...beans or bacon and eggs. That sort of thing." He took another mouthful and savored the taste. He felt eyes on him.

"No wonder you're so skinny," she told him in no uncertain terms. "You're not eating properly."

Seth looked down. He wasn't skinny, he was... Okay, so maybe he was skinny, but it was from the hard work he did on a daily basis. Manual labor didn't allow you to get fat. It also built muscle. As if to prove his point he rolled up a sleeve and flexed his muscles. "I'm not skinny," he said, piercing her with his eyes.

"Oh my," she said, then burst out laughing.

Seth felt heat rise up his face. He felt humiliated but wouldn't tell her so.

She stared at him, and suddenly her laughter stopped. "I'm sorry. I didn't mean anything by it." He nodded. He was too annoyed to speak and filled his mouth with food instead. Inside he was seething, which was stupid. Abigail had been joking, he knew she had, but it still stung. Glancing across at Mabel he saw confusion on the child's face. At least she didn't understand what had just occurred.

Abigail reached out and covered his hand. *I'm sorry*, she mouthed, and he felt a little better. "Eat your supper, Mabel," she suddenly said, then picked up the child's fork and began to feed her.

"I'm tired, Aunty," she said, rubbing at her eyes again. "I want to go to bed."

She began to climb off the chair loaded with cushions, and Seth rushed to her side. He lifted her off, and Mabel looped her arms around his neck, then snuggled in. At first, he wasn't sure what to do. Should he cuddle into her or pull away? He glanced across at his wife for guidance. She said and did nothing, which was no help whatsoever.

Slowly, almost reluctantly, he lifted his arms and wrapped them around the little girl who had put so much faith in him. Seth had already decided not to get attached to the sweet child, since her father could arrive any day to take her away. But already she had stolen his heart, and that just wouldn't do. "Goodnight, sweet Mabel," he whispered, then handed her over to her aunt. Mabel leaned in and kissed his cheek.

"Goodnight Uncle Seth," she said wearily.

His heart filled with love. Is this what it was like to have a child of his own? Having his heart filled with joy? Seth quickly remembered he needed to keep his distance and not get emotionally attached to the tiny tot. Regrettably, it was already too late.

* * *

Reflection of the flames from the fire flickered across Abigail's face as she slept. Seth had watched her on and off for the past hour. The trip to Halliwell had taken some days, and she looked exhausted. Had she been alone, it would have been an arduous journey, but with a small child in tow, it would be far worse, he was certain.

He set his Bible aside and lifted her gently from the chair. They'd not discussed it, but with Mabel sleeping in the spare bed, there was no choice but to place her aunt in his bed. Not that Seth was complaining, and it would be difficult for him, no doubt. But he was an adult, and could keep his thoughts away from a beautiful woman in his bed for one night. He was sure he could.

Seth glanced down into her face. She looked relaxed but weary. In her position, he was certain he would be the same. He shoved the bedding back and lay her down tenderly, then gently removed her shoes. She stirred as he did so but remained asleep. He covered her with the warm eiderdown, then left the room. It would not be long, and he would go to bed himself. After all, he had a long day ahead of him. He was up at the crack of dawn each and every day, so went to bed early each night. Things would be easier now he had a wife to prepare his meals, clean the house, and do his laundry. Mary had helped out where she could, but with a small baby herself, he couldn't ask her to continue.

Abigail was the answer to all his problems. Well, perhaps not all, but she would certainly make his life easier.

Seth returned to the sitting room and poked at the fire, pushing the logs to the back. He couldn't risk having them roll out onto the floor and setting the house alight. For some reason he felt a little awkward. He knew the reason but tried to deny it – there was a stranger in his bed, and he did not want to intrude. It sounded silly, even to Seth. They might be strangers, but they were married; he had the marriage license to prove it.

He sat in the armchair staring at the dwindling fire for some time, then finally decided to bite the bullet. It had been a long day, and he needed to be up early. He stretched himself out as he stood, then decided to check on Mabel. She was in a strange house, a different room, as well as a bed she didn't know. Perhaps Abigail should have slept with Mabel tonight?

Well, it was too late for that now, but had he been thinking, he may have suggested that. Although on second thought, Mabel might have expected it long-term. The fact he'd been forced into this marriage still grated, but if he had to be married, he might as well at least get some heirs out of it. His father would expect that, at the very least. With no heirs, who would inherit his land and his cottage? Father would not be pleased if Seth's share of the land was sold off. Although he could leave it to his brothers' children if necessary.

Seth shook himself. He definitely needed heirs, and he was certain Abigail would agree. Maybe not today, or even next week, but some time in the future. At least he could hope.

Seth finally took himself off to bed. It felt strange having another person in the bed. This was a whole new experience for him. He'd never shared a bed with anyone, not even his brothers. Growing up they each had their own bedroom and their own bed. Despite their father being the richest landowner in the county, he did not allow his sons to sit on their laurels. They had to work for their allowances, and both Noah and Seth worked the land. Jacob was not so inclined, and was more talented in the area of paperwork and accounting. Father even sent him off to learn how to do it properly. Because of this, he had a number of people working his land, including some cousins.

Seth shuddered. Paperwork was the thing he hated the most.

He rolled over and faced his bride who seemed to be in a deep sleep. He'd been so nervous waiting for her to arrive. Not having a photograph of her played with his mind. He worried she would be a hag, but he knew now he had nothing to worry about. Abigail was the most beautiful creature he'd ever set eyes on. He already knew their children would be beautiful too.

Her silky brown hair lay across the pillow, and it took all his willpower not to caress it. It was not the right thing to do, not without her permission. Her mouth twitched and she suddenly groaned then rolled over. There was nothing left for Seth to do now but go to sleep. But with a beautiful woman laying next to him, it was not as easy as it seemed.

Chapter Three

Seth awoke with a start and rolled over. He was alone in the bed - Abigail was already awake and had left the room. Their room. He wasn't sure what had awoken him, but no doubt Mabel was up and playing. He quickly got up and dressed. He'd had a fitful sleep and felt as though he hadn't slept at all. He wondered how Abigail had faired.

He headed for the bathroom where he would smother his face in cold water. If he could douse his entire head in it would be better still, but he didn't have that luxury. The cold water would wake him up and hopefully make him feel a little better.

He stared at his reflection in the mirror. He looked like something from a horror book. The water at least made his hair sit down a little better. Seth knew he could do with a shave, but he'd slept in, and didn't have time.

What would his new bride think if he let himself go like that? He reached for his razor, but it was nowhere to be seen. Splashing a little more water on his face, he dried off then staggered out to the kitchen.

"Something smells good." The aroma hit his senses the moment he entered the room. If he was truthful, even before he reached the kitchen, he could smell it.

"Is bacon and eggs all right? I'll do better tomorrow I promise."

Abigail looked and sounded apologetic, but for what? "I don't usually eat breakfast, especially when I'm running late, like today."

She pierced him with such a look that Seth sat himself down at the table and waited to her to serve him. Upsetting his wife on their first few days of marriage was not a good omen. No, he would have breakfast and then go to work. His foreman knew what needed doing and was more than capable of allocating work. Besides, he knew Seth's new wife was arriving, and probably had all sorts of ideas running through his mind when his boss didn't turn up on time.

"Do you drink coffee, Uncle Seth?"

Mabel was suddenly at his elbow. Seth hadn't seen her move from her spot on the floor where she'd played with a worn-out doll. "I certainly do," he said, staring down into the face of his new niece. "I like it strong and black." Not that it meant anything to Mabel, because at

A Bride For Seth

four-years-old, the child would not be serving him coffee.

"I knew that already," Abigail said as she carried his breakfast to him. She placed a mug of coffee on the table, and a plate full of bacon and eggs. Far more food than he'd expected.

"There's enough here to feed a small army." He glanced up at her. Did she really expect him to eat all this food when he normally didn't consume breakfast? The look on her face told him she did.

"As I understand it, you do manual labor. You need to have a decent meal at the start of each day." She smiled at him, and Seth couldn't say no.

"What about you and Mabel?"

"We had breakfast when you were asleep, silly." Mabel's mirth-filled voice came from beside him, and he felt guilty for sleeping in while the pair had been up far earlier.

"Eat up, then you can go to work and get out of my hair." She grinned at him, and he knew she was joking. If he'd been thinking, he would have arranged to take some time off for a few days. After all, he had a new bride, and the way things were right now, he wouldn't see much of her. They needed to get to know each other to make their marriage work.

"Maybe I should stay home today." The moment the words were out she scowled.

"Don't you trust me?" Now she looked hurt.

"I...no, that isn't it at all. Despite marrying by proxy some weeks ago, we are complete strangers. I thought perhaps we should get to know each other better. Besides, you arrived with almost no luggage. Maybe we should go into town and get some clothes for you both. You could make a shopping list for food?"

"I lived on a ranch before I came here. I know how things are done, and that's not it. Go to work and make arrangements with your foreman. Perhaps tomorrow we can go to town?"

Of course, she was right. He nodded then stared down into his plate, snagging a piece of bacon onto his fork. Abigail placed four slices of toast next to him, and he inwardly groaned. If he had pigs, they would have a great feed today. Since he didn't have any, he'd have to eat the food himself.

Little eyes watched his every move, but Seth tried not to let it bother him. He wasn't used to being watched, at least not in his own home. He figured both he and Mabel would have to learn about each other, and perhaps this was the way four-year-olds accomplished that.

He glanced down at her and smiled, then pushed his plate away. "I can't eat any more. I'm sorry." Mabel stared up at him open-mouthed from where she played on the floor with her rag doll.

"You have to eat it all. Aunty says so." She glanced across at her aunt, a worried look on her face.

Abigail had her hand across her mouth, obviously trying to disguise her laughter. He saw through her, but did her niece? She suddenly straightened her shoulders and wore a blank expression. "It's fine, Mabel. I didn't know how much Uncle Seth could eat, so I might have given him too much."

Little eyes stared up at him, and she whispered loudly, "You're lucky this time."

His heart fluttered. Mabel was a sweet girl. She didn't deserve what life had dished out to her.

"I must go now," he said as he stood. He was about to carry his dishes to the sink when they were whisked out from under him. "I can do that," he said. His wife would not become his slave, of that he was certain.

She smiled sweetly. "It's fine. You get yourself ready for work."

He looked down at his work clothes. Did he look *that* bad? "I'll wash up and then I can leave."

Once he was cleaned up, Seth headed for the door, just as he did every other morning. Only today he was not alone, and almost too late he realized he needed to say goodbye. "I'm off," he called to Abigail. She scurried out of the kitchen, wiping her hands on her apron, one of the few items she'd brought with her.

She leaned into him and offered up her cheek, which confused Seth for a moment, but then he kissed the proffered cheek. She stared into his eyes, and Seth had difficulty pulling his away. Until he felt tugging on his breeches.

"Uncle Seth, what about me?" He glanced down to see two little arms upward, waiting for him to pick her up. He couldn't say no to such a generous offer and picked Mabel up. She promptly put her arms around his neck, then gave him a big sloppy kiss.

His grip tightened and his heart filled with joy. All thoughts of keeping his distance from his new little niece suddenly vanished.

Chapter Four

Abigail glanced at the young woman standing at her door. She had no idea who the stranger was, but she sure was pretty. She noticed the rosy cheeks first, no doubt from the chill in the air. Her blonde hair was pulled back into a braid.

Before Abigail could utter a word, something was shoved into her hands. "Do you mind?" the unknown visitor said. "It's difficult juggling a cake and the baby at the same time." Until that moment, she hadn't noticed the small baby in her arms. The past few days had been so traumatic, and had gone past in such a whirlwind, Abigail hadn't really noticed. The babe wasn't very old – a few months at most.

When she glanced up again, a huge grin lit the face of the other woman. "I'm Mary – Noah's wife." Abigail was still quite bewildered and stared at the woman. "Your sister-in-law. Noah is Seth's brother – you would have passed our cottage on your way here."

Abigail felt the heat rise up her neck and face, embarrassed that she did not know who the woman was standing before her. "I'm sorry. It was a long trip, and..."

"Please, don't be sorry."

Abigail opened the door wider and let her new sister-in-law in. "Please sit down," she said, stretching to see the small baby in Mary's arms. "Who might this be?" She felt a flutter in her heart. She had a niece or nephew. She tried not to think about the nephew she'd recently lost.

"This is Eugene. He's only a few months old."

Mabel suddenly ran into the sitting room, no doubt curious about the chatter she could hear. "A baby! I love babies," she almost cried, so excited at the prospect of a baby being in their new home.

"Shhh. Don't frighten him." Abigail pulled the little girl closer, then picked her up to look into the baby's face. "Isn't he beautiful?"

"He is," Mabel said with tears running down her face.

"This is your Aunt Mary, and baby Eugene is your cousin," she said gently.

"Can I hold him?"

"I don't think so, Mabel," Abigail said. He's a tiny baby and might get hurt. Besides, you are way too excited to hold him."

Mabel looked disappointed, but only for a matter of seconds. "Is that cake? Can I have some?"

Abigail straightened her shoulders. "Where are your manners, young lady?" Her stern voice pulled Mabel up.

"I'm sorry, Aunty. Can I have some cake *please*?"

When she glanced up, Mary was forcing back a smile. "It's carrot cake," Mary said. "Do you like carrot cake?"

Mabel stuck out her tongue and feigned being ill. "Mabel Merriman, that is very rude. Any more bad behavior and you'll spend the rest of Aunt Mary's visit in your room."

"I'm sorry, Aunt Mary," she said, and sat on the floor at her new aunt's feet. As close as she could possibly get to Eugene, Abigail decided.

"I'll make us a drink. Tea or coffee?" she asked Mary.

"Tea, thank you. Can I help?"

Abigail glanced across at her nephew. "You stay there – I'll be perfectly fine." Abigail already felt a connection to Mary. She was nice, she was kind, and she was now family.

"Tell me about yourself," she said when Abigail returned with the refreshments. She'd cut the cake, and

Cheryl Wright

Mabel glanced at it, not saying a word. At least not to begin with.

"Can I *please* have some cake," she almost begged.

Abigail smiled and glanced at the child. "I thought carrot cake was horrible."

"I don't know," she said as she pouted. "I haven't had any."

Mary raised her eyebrows, and Abigail knew she'd played the situation well. It was a lesson Mabel would long remember. She handed a plate over, and Mabel shoved a small piece of cake into her mouth. "It's yummy," she said as a second piece went in.

"Yes, it is. Thank you, Aunt Mary, for bringing us cake."

When they had finished their refreshments, the women talked about anything and everything. Mary wanted to hear Abigail's story, and nothing was held back. It was all Abigail could do not to cry at the situation Mary had come from. One thing was certain, they had both been saved by the changed will their husband's father had left.

* * *

Abigail glanced around the *Halliwell Mercantile*. It was far bigger than the mercantile back home, and stocked more products too. Most of the time she had to order what was required, apart from the staples for cooking.

Seth came up behind her, his arms creeping around her. Their eyes locked and she wanted to kiss him right there, but propriety being what it was, that was out of the question. A shudder went through her as he caressed her cheek. Last night she'd become Mrs Seth Adams in every way, and she wasn't complaining. Seth had been gentle with her, as she knew he would. She'd worried about their coupling, but it wasn't terrible as she'd envisaged.

"What about this gown?" Elizabeth Dalton, the mercantile owner's wife, had a booming voice and startled her out of her musings.

"She'll need at least three," Seth cut in. "And the same for Mabel." He wandered off and left them alone, and Abigail felt suddenly cold without his warmth next to her.

Her niece looked up excitedly at the prospect of new clothes. "Am I getting a new gown?" The glee on her face was plain to see, and she twirled about on the spot.

"Yes, Sweetheart. Uncle Seth is being very generous and buying new clothes for both of us." Mabel clapped her hands together, then wandered over to her uncle.

Elizabeth glanced up and studied Abigail, and she squirmed under the attention. "Seth is a kind and generous man. You'll see."

She already had. Seth was far more than she had anticipated. Abigail suddenly turned at her niece's scream, but she need not have worried. Seth held her in his arms and handed Mabel a new doll.

"For me?" Tears filled the child's eyes. "Thank you, Uncle Seth." She leaned forward and hugged him tight.

"She already has a doll," Abigail said under her breath.

"Let him spoil her," Elizabeth said quietly. "The Good Lord sent you both to him, and until now he's had no one except his brothers."

"Mabel won't be staying. Her father will collect her when he's back to his normal self." Abigail was firm on this. As much as she would love Mabel to be with them forever, it just wasn't possible.

Abigail was suddenly off-balance. "No running," Seth said firmly. "You almost knocked Aunty off her feet." He scowled at the child and she stepped back. "Are you all right?" His words were directed at Abigail this time.

"I'm fine. She already has a doll. You must have seen her playing with it."

Seth glanced down at Mabel, who was playing with her new toy. "I know, but it's old and falling apart. This is a special gift to welcome her to my home. Our home."

Abigail leaned in and lowered her voice. "You know she's not staying. When Pete…"

Seth stared at her with pity in his eyes. "If he comes to collect her," he said. "How do you expect him to work with a small child to care for?"

"He'll work something out." Abigail knew he was right but didn't want to think about it. Mabel needed her parents, and now Pete was all she had left. Seth shrugged his shoulders but didn't seem convinced.

Once their shopping was done, Seth loaded up the wagon. Abigail worried over the size of the account but had little money to contribute. She reached into her pocket and pulled out everything she had, which wasn't much, just a few dollars.

"Don't you dare take that." Seth's voice boomed from the door. "Put your money away, Abigail." He was angry with her. "I have more than enough to support you and Mabel, and nothing else to spend my money on." He came to stand beside her, and his arms reached around her, pulling her close.

"Why are you angry, Uncle Seth?" The small voice sounded scared, and that was the last thing Abigail wanted. She knew Seth wouldn't want it either.

"Uncle Seth isn't angry, just a little upset," Abigail said gently.

Mabel suddenly dropped the doll to the floor. The movement wasn't lost on Seth, and he stared at it for long moments. He suddenly scooped the girl and doll up off the floor. "I'm sorry," he said gently. "I didn't mean to scare you. Here's your doll – she's yours forever." Mabel snatched the doll from him and snuggled into his shoulder.

"I'm hungry," Mabel suddenly said. "When's lunch?"

The tension in the air suddenly dissipated, and Seth smiled. "That's a great idea. Would you like to go to the diner?"

"What's a diner," she asked. Seth turned to Abigail in question, but before she could respond, he answered.

"A diner is a place to get lunch. Or supper. Or even just a piece of yummy cake." Her eyes sparkled, and Abigail knew the earlier awkward situation was already forgotten.

"I've never been to a diner, I think," Mabel said, and Seth glanced her way. It was a sad indictment of their difficult lives. Grace and Pete barely survived week to week, which was another reason she'd decided to leave. As foreman on a large property, they should have been well off, but with Pete's gambling, there was never enough money. Abigail wanted to get a job to help out, but Grace begged her not to – who would look after Mabel if she had to go to work each day? "Have I, Aunty?"

"No, you haven't, Sweetie." It made Abigail sad, even knowing it wasn't her fault.

"Then let's go," Seth said, and they headed for the door.

Chapter Five

Mabel couldn't sit still – this visit to the diner was a big adventure for her. Seth wondered what their lives had been like before they'd arrived in Halliwell. Not that he was judging, far from it, but Abigail hadn't talked much about her life prior to their marriage, and he got the impression things weren't all that good. They'd arrived with few possessions, including clothes. He wasn't sure if it was because they'd left in a hurry, or simply didn't own much. He was leaning towards the latter.

"Don't do that, Mabel. Can't you just sit quietly?" Abigail was getting agitated with her niece, but the child was probably feeling overwrought. She'd arrived at a strange place only days ago, met a stranger and lived in his house, and now had been brought to yet another strange place. All things considered, Seth thought she'd done quite well.

"Come and sit with me, Mabel," he said gently. "We'll look at the menu together." He outstretched his arms, and she hesitated momentarily until Abigail nodded her approval. Then and only then, the child came running. Seth lifted her onto his knee, then lifted the menu.

"What's a menu," she asked, glancing up at him. His gut churned. Mabel had missed so much in her young life. As he glanced across at Abigail, she paled.

"It's not your fault," he said quietly, then reached across and covered his wife's hand before turning to Mabel.

"This is a menu," he said, looking down at the young girl. "It tells us what food the diner has for us to eat." She turned to the menu, but of course, couldn't read a word. "Do you like chicken? Or beef, or what about fish?"

She shook her head sadly. "I like cake," she said, brightening up.

"Mabel Merriman!! You like all those things." Her aunt scolded her, Mabel turned to Seth.

"I really, really do like cake."

It was all Seth could do to stop himself from laughing. "Since it's such a special day, your first time in a diner, we can probably get some cake for you." He grinned at Abigail, then winked. "Just this once," he added, since his wife was scowling at him.

Mabel clapped her little hands then turned to hug him. "Thank you, Uncle Seth," she said as she wrapped her arms around him. Seth's heart fluttered. He'd promised himself to keep his distance, knowing his new niece wouldn't be with him for long. But his heart was so full of love for her, and he had no idea how he would cope when she eventually went back to her father to live.

It was the last thing he wanted to think about. In the meantime, he could make Mabel's life a happy one while she was with him. Making her happy was making him far happier than he'd been in a very long time.

"The food here is delicious." Abigail wiped her mouth with the cloth napkin. "Thank you for bringing us here, and for spoiling Mabel."

"She deserves to be spoiled," he whispered as he glanced down at her. Mabel sat on the floor playing happily with the new doll Seth had brought for her. "And while she's with us, I'll continue to spoil her." What his wife would think of that, he had no idea, but he wanted the little girl to enjoy her time with her aunt and uncle. He didn't want her to look back on it and remember it as a time she was particularly unhappy.

Seth drank down the last of his coffee. His belly was full, and his heart was happy. They'd already had a big day, and Mabel's energy was beginning to wane. If he was truthful, Seth's was too. His little niece never stopped, and it was draining chasing after her all the time. He honestly had no idea how Abigail did it.

"If you're ready, we should go," Seth said. Mabel glanced up at him with sad eyes.

"Do we have to?"

"Yes, we do," Abigail told her. "It's been a very long day, and it's past time for your nap.

"But I'm not tired," she said, barely keeping her eyes open. Seth barely held back a laugh. He leaned down and scooped the sleepy child up, holding her against his shoulder. She was asleep before they left the diner.

"She's a determined little mite," he whispered.

Abigail nodded. "I'm going to miss her when she's gone." He knew exactly how she felt. His life had changed so much in the past days, and now he couldn't imagine life without his two girls in it. He suddenly felt hollow, and he knew he was already anxious about his niece's departure. If he was this apprehensive, how would Abigail be feeling? She must be devastated.

No matter what either of them thought, it wasn't their choice. Her father would arrive soon and take his daughter back home. She needed to go where she belonged, no matter what they thought. He resolved there and then to step back and not get attached to young Mabel. Unfortunately, Seth knew it was already too late. His heart was already full of love for her. The sooner she left the better, especially for Abigail who was far too attached to the child already.

He helped his wife up onto the wagon, passed Mabel up, then climbed up himself. They were not long out of town when he felt Mabel resting against him. His hand automatically went down and patted her. His heart did a flip. What happened to keeping his distance? He suddenly pulled his hand back, and Abigail glanced at him. Did she know what was running through his mind? If he wasn't wrong, she was thinking along the same lines.

Chapter Six

Noah, Mary, and baby Eugene arrived for the family dinner Abigail had arranged. It was her first-time cooking for so many people, but she did the best she could. The table had been set ready for their visitors, and Mabel was curious about the entire situation.

"Why is the table like that," she asked.

Abigail glanced down at her. "Because we're having visitors."

"What are visitors?" she asked.

They never had visitors at their old house, so it was understandable she had no idea what it meant. "People who don't live at our house."

Mabel's eyes opened wide. "Why don't they?"

Normally her gabble didn't bother Abigail, but today she felt unable to cope with the constant chatter.

Instead, she felt stressed and far from capable of entertaining Seth's family, most of whom she'd never met. Of course, she knew Mary and Eugene, but this would be her first-time setting eyes on Noah and Jacob, his brothers.

"Sounds like they're here," Seth called from the bedroom where he was tidying himself up.

Abigail straightened herself up and removed her apron. She checked Mabel over and ensured she was clean and tidy. "Remember what I said about behaving," she warned her niece. "No one likes a naughty child."

"I promise, Aunty," Mabel said, then moved in for a hug. Seth entered the room and swept the girl up into his arms. Abigail loved that he treated Mabel like his own child.

He opened the front door and welcomed their guests. "Come in, come in," he said brightly. "Mabel, this is your Uncle Noah," he said as his brother moved closer. Mabel snuggled into his shoulder, covering her face. He chucked her under the chin. "He won't hurt you. At least say hello."

Noah grinned at her antics. "Remember what I said, Mabel." Abigail turned to Seth. "She's not usually this shy." Noah was gracious and seemed unconcerned about his new niece's refusal to acknowledge him. "A lot has happened recently," she said. "I'm Abigail." She extended her hand.

Noah took her hand then pulled her in and hugged her. "Welcome to the family," he said gently, and Abigail's emotions were almost overwhelming.

"Oh, here comes Jacob," Seth said. "Another uncle for you, Mabel."

"Too many uncles!" she almost shouted. Seth grinned, and Mabel glanced toward the door then tucked her head into Seth's chest again. He patted Mabel's back, trying to calm her.

Abigail knew exactly how her niece was feeling. Even as an adult she felt overwhelmed. Seth was really the only person she knew. She'd met Mary of course, but their acquaintance was quite brief so far. "Everyone, come in and sit down at the table. Supper is almost ready," she said, heading toward the kitchen.

"Wait," Seth said gently. "Let me introduce everyone." He cocked his head to the side, then reached for her. "Are you all right," he asked quietly so the others couldn't hear.

With Seth supporting her Abigail felt far better, but butterflies churned in her stomach. She thought meeting her new husband would be difficult, this was far harder.

Once the introductions were over, everyone sat at the table as instructed. Mary handed over a cherry pie, and Abigail took it into the kitchen. "Thank you, Mary. That was lovely of you." She leaned forward and hugged her new friend, who happened to also be her sister-in-law.

"It's nothing," Mary said. "You must be feeling overwhelmed, and I wanted to do something to help."

Abigail looked to the floor. "A little, but I'm more concerned about Mabel. It might be too much for her."

"Then we'll keep an eye on her," Mary said, and Abigail nodded. Mary must have been in this same situation when she arrived, so she would understand. The women carried the food to the table, and Mabel's eyes opened wide.

"This is your new family, Mabel," Seth said, holding her on his knee. Abigail watched as she glanced around the table.

"Where's baby?" she suddenly demanded, which told Abigail she had remembered Mary from her previous visit.

"He's asleep on the bed."

"My bed?"

Seth chuckled. "Not your bed. Where Aunty Abigail and I sleep."

"Oh."

The women sat down, and Mabel moved to her own chair. Seth had built a high chair to bring her up to the height of the table, and strapped her in.

"Are we all ready to say grace?" Seth didn't wait for an answer, but linked hands with Mabel on one side of him, and Abigail on the other.

"Can I say it, Uncle Seth?" Abigail wasn't surprised at her request, as Mabel loved to say grace. The other adults stared in disbelief, as if they expected a heap of babble. They were in for a surprise.

"Bless this food and..." She faltered and Abigail knew it was because there were strangers watching her. She had never wavered before.

Mabel's eyes filled with tears. Abigail reached over and squeezed her hand. "Why don't you start again?" she said gently.

Seth leaned forward and wiped the tears from her little face, and Mabel took a deep breath. "Bless this food and everyone sitting at this table. Amen." This time the words were said far more slowly and came out perfectly.

When Abigail glanced up, the adults were beaming, and warmth filled her.

"That was wonderful, Mabel," Mary told her, and the others agreed.

"Aunty teached me," Mabel said, and the adults all chuckled.

"Tuck in everyone," Seth said, and they did. Abigail dished up Mabel's food, but she was far too busy checking out her new aunt and uncles to eat. Tonight, she would get a pass, but tonight only. Abigail knew for sure she would eat dessert, so her little belly would be filled.

A feeling of foreboding suddenly filled Abigail. The pair had not missed a meal since arriving at Broken Arrow Ranch. Would that continue? Mabel was certainly sleeping better since they'd arrived, and that might be in part because she had her own bed. Previously the two had shared a bed.

A shudder ran through her just thinking about their past living arrangements. Not to mention the situation they were in. If it hadn't been for her sister and Mabel, she would have left long ago, but couldn't leave them to fend for themselves against Pete.

Then again, where would she have gone?

"Abigail, are you all right?" Seth's voice close to her ear brought her out of her own thoughts. "You've gone quite pale."

She glanced across at him to see his blue eyes studying her. "I'm fine, I promise." He continued to stare. "Maybe a little nervous."

"No need to be nervous. We're all family, and family look out for each other."

Abigail wished that were the case. Who was looking out for her sister and Mabel when they needed help? Absolutely no one. She shivered. Tonight was for celebrating, not going over the past. She suddenly reached for Seth's hand and held it tight. "Thank you for letting Mabel and I stay with you."

He looked confused. "Of course you would stay – you're my wife. And Mabel is my niece. She is welcome anytime."

Only Abigail wasn't convinced he really felt that way. He seemed to be holding back when it came to her niece. It was almost like Seth didn't want to get close to her. Was he afraid of children? Or… was he simply afraid to become attached? It was a question that only Seth could answer, and right now, she didn't want to ask that question of him.

She glanced around the table, studying each of their guests one-by-one. Everyone seemed happy, and the food was being eaten. After the stress of living with Pete and his unpredictable moods, it was good to finally be somewhere less difficult, where she was appreciated, and where she knew where the next meal would come from.

Chapter Seven

Seth sat back and patted his belly. "I don't think I could eat another thing," he suddenly declared.

Mabel leaned in conspiratorially and whispered loudly. "Aunty made apple pie," she said, eyes opened wide as though shocked that he might not eat dessert.

Mary looked at her as though she was the cutest child ever, and his brothers chuckled. She really was a sweet child. Sweet and innocent. Every moment he spent with her, she filled his heart a little more. As much as he tried to deny it, Mabel had already gotten under his skin. What would he do when she left? What would Abigail do — would she even cope with the loss? They had a hard road ahead of them, of that he was certain.

Mary suddenly shoved back her chair and began to clear the table, helping Abigail at every turn. He was very appreciative, as his new wife must be feeling out of place, perhaps even a bit lonely. In the short time she had been here, Mary was the one who visited. He really appreciated it. He had liked Mary from the start, and that had never faltered.

The two women were huddled together in the kitchen, laughing and talking: thick as thieves. It was nice to see them getting along so well. It meant he need not worry about Abigail being lonely or feeling isolated out here so far from town.

"Dessert has arrived," Mary announced, carrying the cherry pie she'd brought with her, as well as a bowl of clotted cream.

"Thank you for the cream, Jacob," Abigail said quietly, glancing across to her brother-in-law.

"It was nothing," Jacob said as he grinned. His brothers grinned with him and he shrugged. "It was our cousin Floyd, who also happens to be my foreman. He sent it over."

"Then please thank Floyd for me," Abigail said, placing some bowls on the table. She dished up slices of pie into each bowl – some with cherry pie, and others with apple pie. It all looked delicious to Seth.

"Thank you, Abigail, for a wonderful meal, and you also Mary, for the cherry pie."

When the meal was over, the men sat around chatting and Mabel played quietly on the floor with her dolls. "She's a sweet girl," Jacob said quietly. "It's a real shame what's happened."

Seth glanced up to check the women were out of earshot. "It's terrible," he said when he was convinced Abigail couldn't hear. "From the little I have learned so far, they're best out of there. It's a tragedy what happened to the mother." His brothers nodded their heads in support.

"Coffee anyone?" Abigail approached with two coffees on a tray, and Mary carried the third. "I have an orange cake if anyone would like an extra dessert?"

They all groaned. "I can't fit another bite," Jacob said as he rubbed his belly. "That's the most food I've eaten for a very long time."

"Yeah, since the last time you ate at our place," Noah said, laughing.

"Can I help it if I can't cook to save my life?"

"Sounds like you need a wife," Abigail said, and all eyes turned her way. Seth watched as heat crept up her face.

"Jacob is the next to be married," Seth explained. "For some reason, Father left him until last." Which was probably a good thing, or he might not have married Abigail. "He's the oldest of us, but he is last on the list." It didn't make sense to any of them, but it is what it is.

"I'm tired," Mabel said, rubbing her eyes.

Seth strode over and picked her up. "Say goodnight to everyone." She huddled into his shoulder.

"Goodnight Mabel," everyone said, but she didn't say it back, her shyness taking over. He carried her into the bedroom and Abigail followed.

"I'll get her settled," she said, and began to help Mabel undress for bed. "I'll be out soon."

Seth leaned in and kissed the tired girl's forehead. "Goodnight Mabel," he said, then turned to leave. He hadn't even reached the doorway and she was sound asleep, clutching onto her two precious dolls. He could easily get used to this but knew she wouldn't be staying long. His heart thudded at the thought.

Chapter Eight

Three weeks had passed, and Pete still hadn't arrived to collect his daughter. Not that Abigail wanted her to leave, but it bothered her. She loved Mabel more than anything in the world, but she should be with her Pa. What on earth was the man thinking? He'd suffered a great loss, but so had Abigail. Her sister and nephew had died, and she was still in mourning, as Pete would be. But of them all, Mabel had to be the focus.

Seth was a wonderful husband and uncle. He'd built a small chicken coop and bought a handful of chickens so that Mabel would have that experience. Of course, it also meant they had fresh eggs every day, so it wasn't entirely selfless. He'd made sure to spend time with both her and Mabel every day, coming home well before Mabel went to bed.

"Look Aunty," Mabel said, throwing food toward the chickens. "They like it." Her little eyes opened wide when a few chickens came rushing toward her. "Shoo, go away," she said, ending with a squeal, and backing up to her Aunt. She then ran behind her and clutched her skirts.

"They won't hurt you; they just want the food." Seth's voice came out of nowhere. "Throw the food over there," he said, pointing away from Mabel, so she did. Of course the chickens followed the food.

"What are you doing home? I didn't expect you for hours," Abigail said, somewhat perplexed.

"Can't I visit my girls?" He strolled over and took his wife in his arms. It felt nice being here like this, but what if she had to leave to look after her niece when Pete came back? With her sister gone, there was no way Pete could work and care for Mabel. On the other hand, she was a married woman and needed to stay with her husband. She felt so torn, and the longer Pete stayed away, the more invested she became in her marriage. Seth was a good man and wanted nothing but the best for her and Mabel. He treated them both like royalty.

He was a far better husband than Pete had ever been to Grace, and neither Abigail nor Mabel had wanted for anything since the moment they had arrived at Seth's home. With her brother-in-law, they lived day-to-day, never knowing where the next meal was coming from, or indeed, if there would be a meal. If it hadn't been for the small vegetable patch she'd planted soon after arriving to help her sister shortly before Mabel was born, they would have gone hungry much of the time. She suddenly pulled out of Seth's arms. He stared down into her face. "Is something wrong?" Her eyes filled with tears, but she forced them back, not letting them fall.

"What if I have to leave with..." She dropped her voice so Mabel couldn't hear. "with Pete? If I don't go, who will look after his daughter?" Without her permission, tears flooded her cheeks. Seth pulled her close and wrapped his arms around her again.

"Let's pray it doesn't happen," he said quietly. Abigail nodded but wasn't convinced he even wanted her to stay. There was no mention of not wanting her to leave, nor of his fondness for her, nothing. They hadn't been together that long, but she did feel rather fond of him. More than fond, but he'd voiced no such feelings, and she wouldn't embarrass herself by doing so.

"I don't want to collect the eggs," Mabel said, peeking out from behind her aunt's skirts. "Those chickens are mean." The scowl on her face told Abigail there was little hope of getting her back to the chicken coop again.

Seth dropped his arms and swooped Mabel up, carrying her to the chicken coop. "There aren't any chickens in there," he said, pushing her toward the open gate. "In you go and collect the eggs."

She glanced up at him with tears in her big brown eyes; the same eyes that mimicked Abigail's. They could be mistaken for mother and daughter, and had in fact been mistaken as such on occasion.

"I'm right here behind you," Seth said, glancing about for any stray chickens. "I promise you're safe."

Abigail came up behind her husband, wanting to keep an eye on her niece. She watched as she collected the eggs one by one, and carefully added them to the pocket of her pinafore. Soon all the eggs had been collected and she turned to them and grinned. She looked so very proud of herself, as she should be.

"Well done!" Seth laid praise on her, and Abigail's heart swelled. It was a pity Seth wasn't her birth parent, he did a far better job of looking after Mabel than her own father. Abigail's arms came up around his waist from behind, and his hands slid up to cover hers.

"Thank you," she whispered.

"Of course," he whispered back.

"There are plenty of eggs there," Abigail told her niece. "Perhaps we could make a cake."

The squeal that followed almost pierced her ears. "I love cake!" Abigail was sure Seth liked cake too, so that made three of them.

* * *

"That meal was delicious," Seth said, meaning every word of it. "You know you're spoiling me," he said as he wiped his lips with the embroidered cloth napkin. He'd never been so fancy, but Abigail insisted on getting enough linen to make a set of napkins, and then embroidered every one of them. "I am convinced I'm putting on weight, and it's all your fault," he said, trying to stop himself from grinning.

"Are you complaining?" Abigail stood next to him and leaned in to collect his soiled dishes. Without warning he dragged her on to his lap. "Really, Seth," she said, flicking a napkin at him.

He felt rather playful tonight and liked flirting with his wife. She didn't look too impressed, and he reluctantly let her go. "I have things to do, dishes to wash, and Mabel to put to bed."

He wiggled his eyebrows at her, and she turned away, not letting him see if she was interested or not. Abigail had been a willing participant in their lovemaking since she arrived, and he would never force her if she didn't want him.

She suddenly turned back and grinned. "Perhaps later," she whispered, and his heartbeat accelerated. He glanced down at his niece playing quietly on the floor with her new doll, as well as the old and tattered one. She deserved far more toys, and he planned to buy them for her, whether she stayed or not. There was no reason she couldn't take them with her when she left.

His heart suddenly pounded. Mabel had truly gotten under his skin, and into his heart. She was such a sweet child, and not unlike her aunt. He had tried hard not to get close to Mabel, but his well-thought-out plan had failed. He had a soft spot for her and was certain that would never change.

"Time for bed, Miss Mabel," Abigail told her, and she immediately clutched her dolls to her chest. She didn't complain but jumped up and skipped over to Seth.

"Goodnight Uncle Seth," she said, slipping her arms around his neck to pull him closer. She tightened her grip, then gave him a big sloppy kiss on the cheek. He sure would miss that when she was gone. He almost felt like her Pa at times. Perhaps one day he and Abigail might have children of their own. If he were this entrenched in young Mabel, what would he be like with his own offspring?

Abigail took Mabel by the hand and guided her toward bed. Seth had paperwork to do and headed into his office while his wife settled her niece for the night. By the time he finished up, Abigail had finished tidying the kitchen and finally sat down, joining him not long afterwards. They sat next to the fire for what seemed forever. He read passages from his Bible, and she listened intently. When he glanced across, she'd begun to nod off. Her days were long, and full. No wonder she was tired. He picked her up carefully and took her to bed, laying her down gently.

As he sat on the side of the bed, her fingers made their way up his bare back. Perhaps she wasn't as tired as he'd thought.

Chapter Nine

It was now five weeks since Grace had passed on, and Abigail's heart broke a little more each time Mabel asked when her Ma was coming to get her.

No matter the number of times she explained Grace was not coming back, her niece still couldn't grasp the reality of her mother's death. Instead of persisting, Abigail looked for distractions. Today they'd had full day feeding the chickens, tending to the vegetable garden, baking, and preparing the meals. Mabel loved living on the *Broken Arrow Ranch*, and Seth seemed to love her presence too. The two got on wonderfully.

It had been a long day, and Mabel was already sound asleep. It would not be much longer, and the adults would head to bed too. Early mornings meant early to bed. Not that Abigail was complaining. There was always so much to do with a youngster around.

The warmth from the fire warmed Abigail from her head to her toes. It felt like such a homely thing to do, sit in front of the fire, but she had no idea why.

"Maybe we can visit Noah and Mary tomorrow after church?" Seth's voice startled her, as she'd begun to nod off. "I know Mabel would enjoy that. She adores the baby."

"Sounds good. If it's not too cold, perhaps a stroll afterwards?" She smiled at her husband. "Mabel has settled in well, don't you think?"

"Sometimes I think too well," Seth said, choosing his words carefully. "Does she even realize she won't be staying permanently?"

Abigail sighed. She'd tried to explain, she really had, but at four, Mabel simply couldn't comprehend what it meant. "I honestly don't think so. She seems to think..."

A knock at the door interrupted their conversation. Seth glanced at her, silently asking a question. "I have no idea who it could be," she said, anticipating his words.

He headed to the door, opening it cautiously. "Sheriff Dawson! This is a surprise. Come in." He opened the door wide, and the sheriff's gaze went straight to Abigail who was now standing.

"Seth," he said grimly. "Mrs. Adams." He nodded as he said her name, then moved further into the room. He turned to Seth as if pleading for help. "Why don't we all sit down?"

"Please," Seth said, indicating for the sheriff to sit. Abigail sat too. She was now feeling quite light-headed. For the sheriff to visit at such a late time, it couldn't be good news. Her heart thudded as she waited for him to speak.

"I've had a telegram from Sheriff Blackstone over in Harrison County." He glanced at Abigail. Harrison County is where she lived with her sister. Her heart pounded, and she held her breath. There was only one reason the sheriff from her previous county would contact Sheriff Dawson. "It's about your brother-in-law, Mrs. Adams. Peter Merriman – he's been found dead."

She suddenly stood. "Pete's dead? What am I going to tell my niece?" Her head began to swirl, and the last thing Abigail remembered was her descent to the floor.

When she awoke, Abigail was laying on the bed with a cool cloth on her forehead. Seth sat on the bed next to her. He smiled when she opened her eyes. "Welcome back. Are you feeling any better?"

She reached for the cloth, but he stopped her by covering Abigail's hand. "I'm fine now. I, I was hoping it was all a dream. A nightmare, but it's true, isn't it? Pete's gone."

Seth squeezed her hand. "I'm afraid so."

She swallowed down the emotion that threatened to overtake her. "What will happen to Mabel now? Will they take her away?" Tears filled her eyes, and Seth pulled her to him. "I'm the only family she has now. Poor, sweet Mabel." She cried a river of tears for the little girl she'd practically brought up, and worried on her behalf.

"No one is taking her anywhere. But let's not worry about that tonight. Everything will become clearer in the morning." He caressed her back and held her close. Abigail was too distraught to think about the future, but one thing she did know, was if Mabel was taken from her, she would be shattered.

* * *

Abigail awoke wrapped in Seth's arms. She'd had a fitful sleep, and he'd pulled her close every time she began to sob. She wasn't crying for Pete – he was a poor excuse of a man. It was Mabel she cried for; she'd lost both parents in a matter of weeks. It was utterly heartbreaking, and she had no idea what she would tell the child.

Dragging herself out of bed, Abigail made her way to the kitchen, where she discovered Mabel was already awake and playing with her only toys – the ragged doll she refused to give up, and the new one Seth had bought for her. She sat on the floor in her nightgown and played happily. Abigail hated to interrupt her play but needed to give her the news.

Determined, she headed toward her niece, but Seth pulled her back. "Wait," he said, a thoughtful look on his face. "What difference is it going to make? She still doesn't understand about your sister, and this will only confuse her more."

He was right, of course he was. "What do you propose we do then?" He pulled her aside while he lit the fire, and they were out of hearing of Abigail's niece.

"Leave things as they are? I don't see the harm in it, and if she asks about her father, then tell her." It made perfect sense, and Mabel still didn't understand about Grace, so Seth was probably right. Besides, the main time she'd seen Pete was when he was drunk, and it wasn't a good look. Sometimes it had been downright scary, and Abigail had done her best to shield the child.

Abigail took a deep shuddering breath and went to her niece. "Would you like to visit with Uncle Noah and Aunt Mary today," she asked quietly.

"Can I see baby Eugene?" She glanced up only momentarily from her dolls to ask the question.

"Yes, of course."

Mabel held her dolls against herself, as if hugging them. "I love baby Eugene," she said, then went back to playing again.

Abigail stoked the wood stove, then added some additional wood to get the fire burning far better than it was. She filled the kettle and set it on the stove to boil. Finally, she pulled the frying pan from the cupboard and began to make bacon, eggs, and pancakes for their breakfast.

She mixed the pancakes first and allowed the batter to sit, then made coffee for the adults. Mabel would have a cup of milk.

With breakfast now ready, they all sat at the table, hands linked, and Seth said a prayer of thanks. Then they began to eat. "These are yummy," Mabel said.

"Yes, they are," Seth told her as he took another one from the pile. "Aunt Abigail is a good cook."

"Mama is a good cook too. When is Mama coming back?" Mabel's gaze burned into her, and it was all Abigail could do not to turn away.

"She's not coming back, Sweetheart. Mama's gone to heaven, remember?"

Mabel nodded. "What about Papa? Has he gone to heaven too?"

Abigail and Seth glanced at each other. The question was asked so matter of factly, and Abigail doubted her niece even understood what she'd said. "Yes, Mabel, he has. Papa won't be coming back either."

She stared from one to the other. "All right," she said, then went back to her food.

Seth had warned her it would do no good to explain to Mabel about her father, and he was right. She had totally no understanding of her mother's death, let alone her father's, and probably wouldn't for a very long time.

Chapter Ten

Seth stayed close to Abigail throughout the church service and did not leave her side afterwards. They attended the after-service fellowship in the hall next door and enjoyed a cup of coffee with the other church goers. Mabel played with a few of the youngsters around her age but was never out of sight.

He'd contemplated suggesting they stay home today, with Abigail being so upset, but decided the company would do more good than harm. It seems he was right. Mary and Noah were there with the baby, and when she spotted him, Mabel came running over. She really did love baby Eugene, but little did she know she'd be seeing far more of him than she ever imagined.

"He's beautiful, Mary," Abigail cooed, and Seth knew she would be an amazing mother someday. Not that he needed proof – she'd brought up Mabel, and just look how she turned out. Such a sweet child, but she'd been through so much in her young life already.

"Are you free this afternoon," Seth asked Noah quietly. "There's something we need to talk to you about."

Abigail's eyes met his, and he wondered for a moment if it was too early. He'd always been close to his brothers, and they'd never kept secrets from each other, but perhaps this time he should. He almost missed the small nod she gave him, and he sighed with relief.

"We had planned to come over later today anyway," Abigail said as she caressed the baby's cheek. She contemplated Mary, and Seth wondered what was going through her mind. The two had become friends in the short time since Abigail had arrived, and it warmed his heart. Right now, she could do with a friend.

He watched as she swallowed hard and her eyes swam with unshed tears. He moved closer and put an arm around her waist. "All right?" he whispered. She nodded, but he knew it wasn't true. She was far from fine, and they both knew it.

"Is everything..." Mary didn't get to finish the sentence before Abigail broke away and ran outside.

"Everything is far from all right," he said quietly, then ran after his wife. He knew Mabel would be safe with her aunt and uncle watching her.

He glanced about but couldn't see Abigail anywhere. She had to be there; where else would she go? The only building nearby was the church. Perhaps she gone to the church where she could draw comfort, and that's exactly where he found her. She sat in the front pew with Preacher Joe who listened intently to every word she said. He watched as she wiped tears from her cheeks but didn't go to her. Her conversation with the preacher was private and he had no right to intrude.

He was about to leave, knowing she was in safe hands, when she glanced up and indicated for him to join them. "It's a terrible situation," Preacher Joe said quietly, but using a tone that made you think everything would be all right. "Abigail is understandably upset for the child."

Seth sat next to her and pulled her close but didn't speak. "I'm afraid for her," Abigail said. "What will happen to her now?" He felt her stiffen against him.

"She's not going anywhere," Seth said firmly. How could Abigail think he would ever contemplate sending her away? She was part of their family, and had been from the moment she arrived, even if he had tried to deny his feelings for the sweet child.

The preacher reached out a hand and placed it on Seth's shoulder. "You're a good man, Seth Adams," he said. "Your father would be very proud if he was here now."

Seth felt suddenly emotional. Was it because of the words the preacher had said, or because of the situation that affected Mabel's life? He had no idea, but he unexpectedly felt completely overwhelmed. He nodded to the preacher and pulled Abigail closer still.

Cheryl Wright

* * *

Abigail set about packing up a picnic lunch. Enough for them all, Jacob included. Before leaving the church they'd arranged to meet up at the creek for a picnic lunch and discuss the turn of events. Noah and Mary were unaware of the situation, but she was certain they'd be as upset as she was. Especially Mary, who was fond of young Mabel.

Mabel was excited for this new-to-her adventure, but even more excited to see her young cousin. Eugene was far too young for any interaction, but just the mere fact he was a baby was enough for the four-year-old.

With the sandwiches all packed, as well as the cake, Abigail filled some large glass bottles with water. The water here was far cleaner than they'd had at her sister's home, and for that she was very grateful. She also had to cart it from the well, and now there was running water, which saved her back and shoulders from the weight of it. Pete was always conveniently unavailable whenever his help was needed around the house, and it hadn't taken long for Abigail to see the man for what he really was. Lazy and uncaring. How her sister ever hooked up with him, she would never know, but that was water under the bridge, and couldn't be taken back now.

Would Grace still be alive if she'd never married Pete Merriman? Abigail would never know, but she would never forget the misery on her sister's face when she realized she was dying. "Take care of Mabel," were her last words, and Abigail promised she would. She swallowed back a sob that threatened to take over. The last thing she needed was for Mabel to see she was upset.

She brushed away a stray tear and glanced down at her niece. "We're having a picnic, Mabel. Won't that be nice?" Mabel stared up at her with the biggest grin on her face. "Eugene will be there too." The little girl clapped her hands and danced around the kitchen.

"When can we go?"

"When Uncle Seth is ready. It shouldn't be much longer."

Seth pulled in with the buggy just moments later, and Mabel spotted him through the window immediately. She ran to the window and sat staring, until he came inside. Then she followed him everywhere. "I guess you are waiting to go," he said, glancing down at her. Mabel nodded her head. "Get your dolls, and if Aunty Abigail is ready, we can leave."

He glanced up at Abigail and grinned. "I think she wants to go now," he said quietly. He scooped his niece up into his arms, and grabbed the picnic basket with his free hand. He then handed the child up to his wife before storing the picnic basket in the back of the buggy, along with a blanket for them to sit on.

Abigail knew Seth was trying to make the day a happy one for her and Mabel, but nothing could make this day better. She was almost certain of it.

Seth pulled on the brake to the buggy, and once secured climbed down. Mary and Noah were already there with Eugene, who lay asleep on his mother's lap. Noah greeted them, a quizzical look on his face. Seth shook his head. His brother was being impatient, and would have to wait. Besides, he wouldn't discuss it in front of Mabel. Abigail would probably take the child for a walk while he told his family. It did, after all, affect them all.

Noah held up his arms to take Mabel, and she shied away at first. "Uncle Noah won't hurt you," Abigail said, and the expression on Mabel's face told Seth she'd forgotten her uncle. When recognition finally hit, she reached out and let him help her down.

"Eugene is with Aunty Mary, but he's asleep," Noah said as he put her to the ground. Mabel reached up for his hand, and Noah accepted her offer.

Seth held Abigail by the waist as he lifted her down from the buggy. Her sad expression was not lost on him. Perhaps this wasn't such a good idea to have a family picnic after all. He knew she wouldn't be happy today, but he didn't want her miserable either. They'd agreed his family had to be told, but he now wondered if it was too soon for Abigail, too raw.

It was certainly that – for Abigail at least. For Seth, he didn't know the man, but the sadness the situation would bring to his family was his main concern. Would Mabel even remember her parents when she was older? He very much doubted it, and that was the hardest part of all. He had fond memories of both his parents, and didn't want to ever forget them. Mabel didn't have a chance to store any precious memories of them, and that was incredibly heartbreaking.

"You can put me down now," Abigail whispered, and her warm breath was close to his face. He only had to turn his face slightly and their lips would be close enough for him to kiss her. Only this wasn't the time. Nor was it the place. He stared into her eyes that were clouded with the shimmer of unshed tears. He wanted to pull her to him and never let go. He wanted to make the hurt go away, to promise her everything would be all right. But he couldn't guarantee that. And it wasn't all right, because her sister and nephew were dead, and now her brother-in-law. Almost an entire family wiped out in a matter of weeks. How was she still standing? How was she even functioning? If he was in the same situation, he would be a wreck, he knew he would be feeling totally insane by now. But his wife was a strong woman, and that helped to keep her sane. It was one of the things he'd admired about her.

He put her gently to the ground, and she leaned into him. "I'm not sure I can do this," she whispered as she reached around his waist.

"We'll get through it together," he whispered back. Seth knew they would.

Chapter Eleven

"Aunty," Mabel said as she glanced up at Abigail. They'd gone for a walk along the creek edge while the adults talked. They were on the look out for lots of ducks according to Mabel. Abigail glanced down at their clasped hands. They were linked forever more. Not that Mabel understood that, not now, but one day she would. She was such a beautiful child, so well behaved. "Where are the ducks?" She sounded exasperated, and her aunt fully understood. They'd walked a fair way by now, for a small child anyway, but Seth had assured the pair, ducks did exist. Of course they chose when to appear, and humans had no say in it.

"They should be just around this corner, according to Uncle Seth, so be very quiet." She wiped her errant tears away before Mabel spotted her crying. Without warning, she felt a tug on her hand. Seth was right, they would find ducks at that particular spot, and Mabel wanted to run to them. "Mabel," she whispered. "Remember, keep quiet or you'll scare them. Then the ducks will fly away." She put a finger to her mouth, and Mabel did the same.

"Can I give them the bread now?" Mabel whispered loudly, her expression one of innocence and anticipation – all at the same time.

"You can, but be very gentle so you don't scare them away."

"Aunty Abigail?"

"Yes, Sweetheart?"

"When can I go home to Mama?"

Choking back a sob, Abigail squeezed her niece's hand. "Mama went to heaven, remember?" This was the hardest part, explaining to a four-year-old that heaven meant forever.

Mabel stared at her with big round eyes. "I know, but when will she be home? I miss my Mama." Tears streamed down her little face, and Abigail pulled her niece close.

"I know you do. I miss her too." Abigail couldn't stop her own tears, and felt for the child. "But you like it at Uncle Seth's house don't you?" Her heart thudded. What if Mabel said no? What would they do if she didn't want to stay? Neither Abigail or Seth had thought that far ahead.

She pushed Mabel back and stared into her face. She wiped the little girl's tears away, and Mabel reached out and wiped her aunt's tears. Then she shrugged. "I guess it's all right. But those chickens are scary."

Abigail couldn't help but laugh. She supposed they were scary for a small child. "Well then," Abigail said, "we'll have to do something about that." She pulled Mabel close again and hugged her tight until her niece pushed back.

"Can I feed the duckies now?"

"Of course."

They moved quietly toward the ducks, and the moment Mabel began to throw bread, there was a flurry of activity. They gobbled up the stale bread, and moved closer to the pair. Mabel ran behind her aunt, clutching at her skirts, and that's where she stayed until the flock of ducks became discouraged and flew away.

Mabel was quiet during the walk back to the picnic spot. Had they been gone long enough for Seth to break the news? Abigail worried they would treat her differently now they all knew the entire story – about how her sister and nephew had died, and now Pete. Things would be different now, the family dynamic would change, not only because she was now a part of it, but Mabel was as well.

She wondered how they would all feel about that, and hoped they would be welcomed with open arms. The little interaction they'd had already had proven positive, so she hoped it would continue. They rounded the corner and she could hear the discussion in full

A Bride For Seth

swing, but couldn't make out the words. Mabel pulled her hand out of her aunt's grip, and ran to Seth. "I fed the duckies," she said, wide-eyed. "Then they all flew away."

"That's great," Seth said, then scooped her up into his arms. "Did you have fun?"

"Yes," Mabel said, "but aunty said Mama is never coming home. I miss my Mama." She snuggled into Seth's shoulder and sobbed. He rubbed his hand across her back and soothed his niece, sadness marring his handsome face.

Abigail forced back her own anguish, and glanced around the family group. Mary swiped at her own cheeks, while Noah put an arm around his wife. Noah and Jacob seemed as upset as the women. Seth continued to console little Mabel, while whispering to her. Every now and then she nodded, then snuggled into his shoulder again. Seth would make a wonderful father one day, and already he was the nearest thing Mabel had to a father. He was a far better man than Peter Merriman ever was.

Suddenly Mabel slid out of his grip and ran to her aunt. "Uncle Seth said we can go to town tomorrow to get some new toys."

Seth was suddenly by her side, and his arm slid around her waist. "We could go to the diner while we're there. You like the diner don't you, Mabel?"

She glanced up at him and nodded her little head. Bribery might work for now, but how long would it last? When Mabel realized she was never going back to her the only home she'd ever known, it might be a totally different story.

Chapter Twelve

The trip to town would be a good distraction, but Abigail knew it wouldn't last forever. Seth's plan was to ply his niece with toys, and keep her mind off the situation. He hoped it would help her forget, and that might work for a short time, but it was not a permanent solution. She was after all, an inquisitive four-year-old, who wanted to know everything.

"Why do I have to wear my Sunday best?" Mabel wriggled about as her aunt tried to dress her. "I wore them yesterday." Now she scowled and stomped her foot. When she wanted, Mabel had a mind of her own, and although it didn't show often, she had a bit of a temper.

"Because we're going to town, remember? Uncle Seth promised you yesterday."

"Are we going in the buggy?"

"We are. Do you like riding in the buggy?"

She scowled again. "No, but I like the horseys." A huge grin lit up her face, and Abigail took the chance to secure her bonnet while the child was distracted.

"Is that so?" It was Seth's voice, and he was right behind her. Abigail hadn't heard him enter. "It just so happens, I might have a horse that's about the right size for you."

Abigail gasped. Did he mean what she thought he meant? Surely he wasn't going to teach Mabel to ride? She was far too small. Wasn't she?

Mabel stared at him, not comprehending. "Perhaps one day soon you might like to come and meet our horses. Even pet them."

Her little face lit up, and it made Abigail's heart flutter. Mabel ran to Seth. "Can I pet them now?" He glanced across at Abigail. He had no idea how little minds worked, how they had no sense of time.

"Maybe for a few minutes while Aunty Abigail gets ready." He leaned in and kissed Abigail's forehead and her heart fluttered. Whenever he was close to her, her heart did funny things. Her stomach roiled, but in a good way, and shivers went down her spine. Did her nearness do the same to Seth?

"Go on then, off you go," she said, still reeling from his touch. "I won't be long though."

Seth grabbed Mabel's hand. She was just about jumping, she was so excited to see the horses. Why hadn't he thought to take her to the stables before? She'd been here some weeks now, but it didn't occur to him. He shook his head. It wasn't a big thing for him, but it obviously was for Mabel, and that was the important thing.

As they reached the stables, he reached into the bucket of carrots and grabbed a handful, passing some down to Mabel. "I don't like carrots," she said with a scowl. He chuckled.

"They're for the horses. They love carrots."

Her eyes opened wide. "Really?" She looked down at them, and pulled a face. "They don't taste very nice."

"The horses think so," he said, and continued to lead her into the stables. They walked almost to the end where Old Nellie was housed. She was the most calm of all their horses, and the one he would use to teach Mabel to ride. Assuming Abigail approved. From the look on her face, and her very audible gasp, he wasn't convinced. In his mind, there was no harm in teaching Mabel to ride. Especially since she was going to be living with them, right here on the ranch.

"You need to be quiet, or you might frighten her." He put a finger to his lips.

"Like the duckies?"

"Exactly like the duckies. They can fly away, but horses just get scared."

"I don't want to scare them," she said, almost in tears. Darn, but he didn't mean to upset her.

"It's all right," he said, lifting her up into his arms. "Shhhh, quietly now." He held her up to the top of the stall so she could see the horse. "This is Nellie," he said quietly, then reached out his hand with a piece of carrot. She moved forward and snapped it up. Seth reached out his hand and petted the horse's head. "Do you want to pet her?"

Mabel snuggled into his shoulder, but only momentarily, then turned back to face the horse. "Will it bite me?"

"Nellie is a girl horse, and she doesn't bite. Watch." He reached out his hand again, and Nellie sniffed around for more carrot. Seth reached into his pocket and offered it to the horse, who snatched it up. He petted her again.

Mabel gingerly reached out her little hand, but when Nellie tried to sniff her, quickly pulled it back. "Give her some carrot," Seth said, and placed a large piece in the child's hand.

Nellie moved in and quickly grabbed it, not waiting for it to be offered. Mabel squealed and the horse suddenly backed away. "It's all right, Nellie," Seth said soothingly. "You scared her, Mabel. You have to be quiet and gentle."

"I'm ready when you are," Abigail said behind them. Seth turned to see the silhouette of his wife. With the sun behind her, and the shadows from the stables, she was a sight to behold. Almost majestic looking. Whenever she was near, his heart skipped a beat. His life had more meaning since she'd arrived. He loved his little family, despite the terrible circumstances that brought them to him.

"Come and meet Nellie first." He turned back to the horse, who had come back for more carrots. "This is it Nellie. No more after this," he said chuckling. "You are very spoiled."

Abigail stared into the stall. "Is this the one?" The horrified look on her face worried him.

"Yes, this is the one." He reached out and pulled her close. "Don't worry. I promise she'll be safe. Nellie is very placid. Let's go before it gets too late."

Four was a good age to start teaching a child to ride, and he wanted to begin soon. He wasn't so sure Abigail was going to agree.

* * *

Mabel was in awe. Seth had set her in front of a shelf of toys and told her to take her pick, much to Abigail's disgust. The child needed guidance and love, not to be spoiled. A box was placed next to her, and Mabel grabbed every doll on the shelf and threw them in. "Enough!" Abigail said under her breath. "Mabel, you may *not* have all those dolls. You can choose four toys only." She held up four fingers to ensure her niece understood. She was met with pouting. "Seth," she said turning to him. "This is not appropriate. Mabel needs to understand limits." He met her words with a scowl.

"But..."

"No buts and no excuses. No matter the circumstances, spoiling a child does not help anyone." She was firm on her words, and would be firm in her resolve.

Seth turned to Mabel. "Sorry Mabel, but aunty has spoken. Four dolls it is." He leaned in to Abigail and whispered in her ear. "What about six?" Abigail glared at him. Even four dolls were too much.

When she glanced down again, Mabel had the dolls lined up on the floor, trying to make her final decision. Abigail felt a little mean, but knew Seth had gone overboard because of his love for his little niece. But if he did it today, she'd expect it more, and that wouldn't do. "Which ones are your favorites?"

Mabel's tongue shot out of her mouth and suddenly went sideways as she thought. "They all are," she wailed. "It's easier for me to have them all!"

"Mabel Merriman, you will not be getting them all. Make a decision or I'll make it for you." Mabel burst into tears.

Seth glanced at Abigail sideways. She suddenly felt very mean. Was she being horrible and uncaring? She didn't think so. This was his fault for spoiling the child instead of behaving like a parent and using some control.

She squatted down to her niece's level. "If you take all the dolls, the other little girls will be sad because there will be none for them," she said quietly.

Her mouth suddenly dropped open. "How many can I have?" Abigail held up her fingers again. Her eyes traveled across the dolls laid carefully on the floor. "I want this one, and this one," she said. "and..." She picked up two more dolls and cradled them. "these."

She stood up with her selections and Abigail stacked the remaining dolls back on the shelf. "Don't you ever do that again," she snarled at Seth. "Mabel has to learn limits. She can't have it all." She scurried to the counter, leaving Seth trailing behind. She'd been mad over the years, but decided this incident would be memorable — for all the wrong reasons.

As they left the mercantile, his shoulders slumped, and she felt far more guilty than she knew she should. Seth was upset with her, and no doubt Mabel was annoyed. Since when was doing the right thing something you should feel ashamed about?

Seth led the pair to the diner. Mabel had enjoyed her visit here last time, and frankly, he should have made more time to bring them both here again before this. "Can I have cake, Uncle Seth?"

Abigail's head shot around. "Manners, Mabel."

"Can I *please* have cake, Uncle Seth?"

Seth tried to hide his mirth behind his hand, but Abigail saw right through him. "Perhaps after you've had your main course," he managed to get out.

"You see what happens when you spoil her," Abigail hissed at him. "It is expected all the time." Oh boy, she was so mad and he didn't blame her. He'd tried to make up for Mabel's situation by giving her whatever made her happy, but he understood now that wasn't how it worked. They'd been getting on so well lately, that he didn't want to spoil things between Abigail and himself. He had to find a way to try and make it up to her.

"Come over here and we'll check the menu," Seth told Mabel, and she came running with her new dolls. "Would you like fish?" She shook her head. "Beef?" Again, she shook her head.

"Just order her scrambled eggs and toast, and Mabel will be happy."

He stared at his wife. "Is that right, Mabel?"

"Then can I have cake?"

"I give up," Abigail said, and Seth could see she was at the end of her tether. The waitress came and took their orders, and his wife still seemed annoyed at him. It was the last thing he wanted.

"Wait here," he said, then left the diner. He arrived back a few minutes later with something hidden behind his back. Seth dropped to one knee in front of Abigail. "I'm sorry for being such a lousy husband and uncle," he said sincerely. "These are for you." He handed her a bouquet of flowers and waited for her response.

Abigail leaned in to better smell the fragrance of the flowers. She glanced up at him, a smile on her face. "Thank you," she said. "You're not a terrible husband or uncle, you're the best. But you do go overboard sometimes."

"I know and I'm sorry. I just want to see her happy."

"She is happy, and totally oblivious to what is going on around her. They are all adult things that a four-year-old can't understand." She reached out and took his hand. "I love you Seth Adams, but you really can be infuriating at times."

Seth almost toppled over. "You love me? I... I have loved you since the day we met, but I didn't think you reciprocated. You have made me so happy in the short time we've been together." He lifted her hand to his lips and kissed it.

Suddenly a little head popped up between them. "I love you too, Uncle Seth," she said, and hugged him tight. How he could ever think he could banish this sweet child from his heart, he would never know. "What's 'fuwiating?'" she demanded.

Epilogue

Mabel sat atop Old Nellie, as she'd begun to call her, waiting for Seth to assist. Truth be told she didn't want to wait, but with her aunt watching her every move, Seth was certain his niece would be less likely to try anything untoward.

She had taken to riding like a fish to water, and Seth couldn't be prouder. He'd planned to buy her a pony for her fifth birthday, but she adored Old Nellie, so for now he would stick with her. Besides, he had heeded Abigail's warning about spoiling the child. Plus he didn't want to get on her bad side again.

"Can we go?" Mabel's frustration came through loud and clear, and it was all Seth could do to stop himself from laughing out loud. Patience was definitely not one of her virtues.

"Hold onto the saddle horn, and we'll get moving soon." She had been a quick learner, which was a blessing. She'd been scared at first, which wasn't a surprise, but she'd calmed down as soon as she realized Nellie wouldn't do her any harm. Even Abigail had taken to the old horse.

Seth was always vigilant about safety, and ensured every part of the saddle was correctly secured and the stirrups were correctly adjusted. Not only did he not want Mabel injured, he ensured Nellie was well protected too.

"When do I get to ride by myself?" Now she was pouting, an unfortunate trait she often used to her advantage.

"Not for a very long time. Isn't that right, Uncle Seth?" Abigail's voice came through loud and strong. She was still a little wary about her niece being atop a horse, but he'd assured her Nellie was safe. He glanced across at his wife and grinned.

Mabel pouted again. "I'm a big girl now – I'm five!" She placed her hands on her little hips and glared.

Seth wasn't sure who the stare was meant for, but it wasn't very lady-like. "I think we have finished for today," he said quietly after a few moments of silence. "Nellie doesn't like badly behaved riders, and neither do I." He reached out to pull the child down, and she had a sudden change of attitude.

"I'll be good, Uncle," she said between crocodile tears. "I promise."

He glanced across at Abigail who nodded her approval. He finished checking the saddle, then reached for the reins. "Let's go, Nellie," he said as they began the long walk out of the stables. Mabel would be a good little rider one day, but for now, she was far too young to go alone. He envisaged some years down the track when she and her siblings would saddle up their horses and go off on long rides. It was such a happy thought it almost brought him to tears. He glanced across at Abigail, who was rubbing at her large protruding belly. He knew this baby wouldn't be their last, and silently thanked his father for his insight. Without the condition of the will, he would still be a bachelor just going through the motions.

"Thank you too, Lord," he said quietly. "Without your intervention, I would not have this beautiful family."

Old Nellie whinnied, and he glanced up to see Mabel pressing her knees into the horse, urging her to go faster. But the old horse was clever. She knew the child needed to go slow. At least until she was far older.

A tear slipped from his eye, and he wiped it away. His life was perfect, and it got better with each waking day.

The End

From the Author

Thank you so much for reading my book – I hope you enjoyed it.

I would greatly appreciate you leaving a review where you purchased, even if it is only a one-liner. It helps to have my books more visible!

~*~

Look out for more books in the Brides of Broken Arrow series.

About the Author

Multi-published, award-winning and bestselling author, Cheryl Wright, former secretary, debt collector, account manager, writing coach, and shopping tour hostess, loves reading.

She writes both historical and contemporary western romance, as well as romantic suspense.

She lives in Melbourne, Australia, and is married with two adult children and has six grandchildren. When she's not writing, she can be found in her craft room making greeting cards.

Links:

Website: *http://www.cheryl-wright.com/*

Blog: *http://romance-authors.com/*

Facebook Reader Group:
https://www.facebook.com/groups/cherylwrightauthor/

Join My Newsletter:

https://cheryl-wright.com/newsletter/

CPSIA information can be obtained
at www.ICGtesting.com
Printed in the USA
LVHW081945231222
735681LV00010B/526